The story of the Tiger Child comes from Orissa in India. The idea that animals once cooked their food is a common theme in myths throughout the world. They generally have their fire stolen from them by men, and are forced to eat food uncooked for evermore.

PUFFIN BOOKS

Published by the Penguin Group
Penguin Books Ltd, 80 Strand, London WC2R 0RL, England
Penguin Putnam Inc., 375 Hudson Street, New York, New York 10014, USA
Penguin Books Australia Ltd, 250 Camberwell Road, Camberwell, Victoria 3124, Australia
Penguin Books Canada Ltd, 10 Alcorn Avenue, Toronto, Ontario, Canada M4V 3B2
Penguin Books India (P) Ltd, 11 Community Centre, Panchseel Park, New Delhi – 110 017, India
Penguin Books (NZ) Ltd, Cnr Rosedale and Airborne Roads, Albany, Auckland, New Zealand
Penguin Books (South Africa) (Pty) Ltd, 24 Sturdee Avenue, Rosebank 2196, South Africa

Penguin Books Ltd, Registered Offices: 80 Strand, London WC2R 0RL, England

www.penguin.com

First published 1996
7 9 10 8

Copyright © Joanna Troughton, 1996

The moral right of the author/illustrator has been asserted

Filmset in Monotype Baskerville

Made and printed in Italy by Printer Trento Srl

A CIP catalogue record for this book is available from the British Library

ISBN 0–140–38238–0

FOLK TALES OF THE WORLD

A FOLK TALE FROM INDIA

THE TIGER CHILD

RETOLD AND ILLUSTRATED BY
JOANNA TROUGHTON

DUTTON

PUFFIN

Long ago the Tiger used to cook his food. One day his fire went out. So the Tiger had to go to the village to fetch some more fire.

The people were frightened when they saw the Tiger coming. They locked their doors and bolted their windows.

The Tiger went back to the jungle. He visited his sister. She had a small tiger cub.

"Go to the village and fetch me some fire," said the Tiger to his nephew. "You are so small, the people won't be afraid of you."

The Tiger Child started off. But on his way he . . .

. . . played with the monkeys . . . splashed in pools . . .

. . . climbed up trees. By the time he reached the village, he had forgotten what his uncle wanted.

"I have come for the thing my uncle wants," said the
Tiger Child. "But I can't remember what it is."
"Is it a bowl of fresh milk?" the grandmother asked.
The Tiger Child drank the bowl of fresh milk.
When it was all gone he said, "No, I don't think it was that."

"I have come for the thing my uncle wants," said the
Tiger Child. "But I can't remember what it is."
"Is it a delicious fish?" the young boy asked.
The Tiger Child ate up all the delicious fish.
"No, I don't think it was that," he said.

"I have come for the thing my uncle wants," said the
Tiger Child. "But I can't remember what it is."

"Is it a soft cushion?" the little girl asked.
The Tiger Child lay on the soft cushion.
"No, I don't think it was that," he said.

"I have come for the thing my uncle wants," said the Tiger Child. "But I can't remember what it is."

"Is it a fine comb for his hair?"
the mother asked.

The mother combed the fur of
the Tiger Child.

"No, I don't think it was that,"
he said.

The Tiger waited all day for his nephew. When the sun set and the stars came out, he went to the village.

The Tiger Child was tired.
He found a house with a
warm fire, and fell asleep.

The Tiger looked in at the window where the
Tiger Child slept.

"You have drunk the fresh milk.

"You have eaten the delicious fish.

"You have lain on the soft cushion.

"You have been combed with the fine comb.

"Now you are asleep by the warm fire.

"Tiger Child, you are not a tiger any more . . .

"You are a CAT!"

The cat woke up. He remembered what his uncle wanted. It was some fire! Then he yawned and went back to sleep.

The Tiger returned to the jungle.
From that time on, tigers have had no
fire. They eat their food raw.

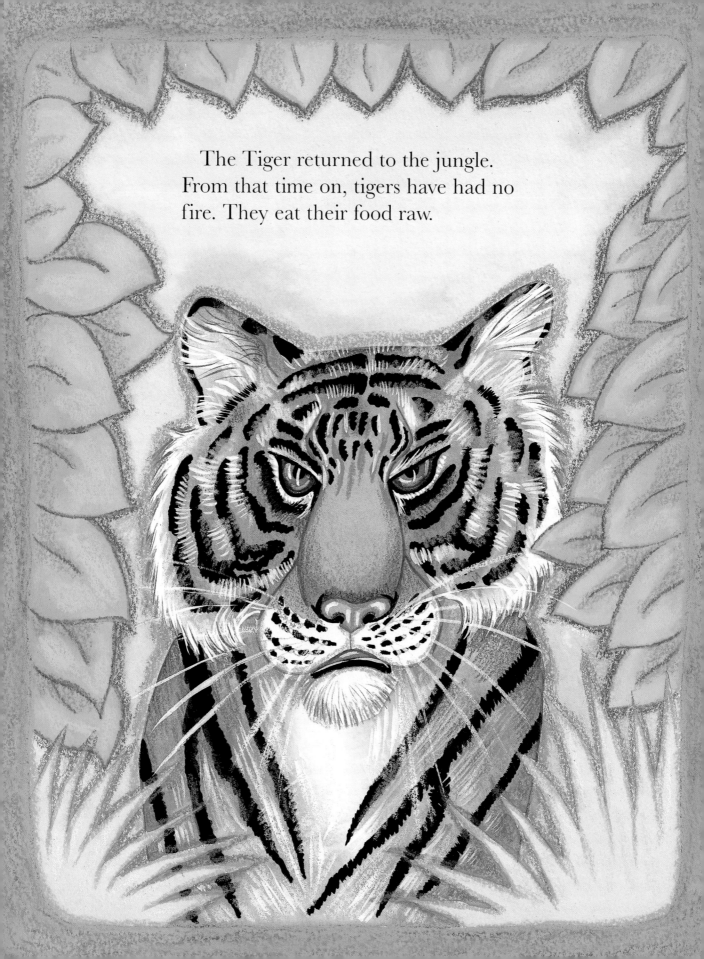

The Tiger Child who turned into a cat stayed in the village.
And cats have lived with people ever since.